I0574257

Merry's PERFECT Christmas

GLORIA BOSTIC

Year of the Book
135 Glen Avenue
Glen Rock, PA 17327

Print ISBN: 978-1-64649-356-2
eBook ISBN: 978-1-64649-357-9

Dedication

To all the family and special friends
who have put the Merry in my Christmases
and the joy in all my days.

1 Merry

"A lovely thing about Christmas is that it's compulsory, like a thunderstorm, and we all go through it together."
                              —Garrison Keillor

Wednesday, December 18

Merry massaged her temple with one hand while pushing her cart with the other and trying to remember, but it was hopeless. She couldn't recall what was on the list she'd left at home and wondered how she was ever going to pull it all together by Christmas day. Remembering the elusive item was impossible, especially with "All I Want for Christmas is You" blaring in the background. Christmas. A once joyful holiday, now a dreaded test she knew she'd fail.

All I want for Christmas is for it to be over. Merry had always loved Christmas above all other holidays—after all, it was also her birthday—but this year would be different, and not in a good way.

With a cart filled with candy canes, new ornaments, and an assortment of things for the Thompsons—a family of four whose angel she'd picked off the tree at her church—she struggled to get down each aisle, maneuvering past the dawdlers, children who should have been left at home, and people who apparently had all day with nothing to do but slow her down.

Merry scanned the shelves, but nothing triggered a memory of that one "impossible to recall" item she knew she was forgetting.

"Oh gawd, I'm getting as bad as Mom was." The thought brought her to a sudden stop, and a shopping cart crashed into the back of her ankles.

"Ow!" Merry glanced at the person behind the cart, ready to accept his apology, especially since she couldn't really blame him, but there was no defense offered.

"You should watch out!" he grumbled as he pushed his cart around and past her. Not so much as a hint of an apology.

"Well Merry Christmas to you," she said loud enough for him to hear. He threw her a strange look over his shoulder, but probably didn't hear her mutter the rest of her thought. "Jerkface!" Not a word from Merry's typical vocabulary—it was a name her teenaged son and daughter often called each other—it just popped into her head and out of her mouth, spurred by utter exasperation.

With the building fear of going down the same path of dementia as her mother—even though she was still a week away from turning forty—pushed aside and having no more energy for the hunt, she gave up and made her way toward the checkout counters, wondering how it had taken over an hour to select the gifts for the family she'd picked off the angel tree. She hoped she'd gotten all the right sizes for everyone and chosen toys that would delight the children on Christmas morning.

When she found the shortest line, one with a mere six people impatiently waiting, she pushed her cart in, and almost ran into the guy in front of her.

Well, wouldn't you know it. It's jerkface! Merry thought he would never believe it was an accident if she rammed into him. As much as part of her would have liked to get even, she knew it wasn't the Christian thing to do, and after all, it had been her fault for putting on the brakes with no warning.

Merry checked her watch every few minutes as she inched her way forward. She pushed her down coat back off her shoulders and mopped the beads of perspiration from her forehead.

Jerkface had finally reached the front of the line and was hurriedly putting his many purchases on the conveyor belt—he was obviously going to make someone's Christmas merry—when he glanced back and saw her. She braced herself for some kind of unpleasant remark, but didn't even get the nasty look she'd anticipated. She couldn't read the man's expression which was fleeting as he turned back to the task at hand, but she did get a better look at him.

Why do all the good-looking ones have to be such jerks? Merry pushed her thick, brown hair behind her ears for the umpteenth time, wondering how it could be thirty degrees outside and so oppressively hot in here.

Though the man wasn't hard to look at, her patience was growing thin watching him place an endless assortment of items on the belt. Merry didn't mean to be nosey, but what else was there to look at? There were colognes—both men's and women's fragrances—notecards and pens, handkerchiefs and scarves, men's socks and sweaters, books, and several boxes of Christmas cards.

It wasn't until he had paid the cashier that he turned to her and sheepishly said, "Hey, sorry about back there. It's been a rough day." Looking embarrassed and not waiting for a reply, he turned and hurried out of the store with his cart full of merchandise.

Merry quickly transferred all her items to the conveyor belt, and as the cashier was ringing out her last item, Merry remembered. "Tape!"

"Excuse me?" the bored and weary looking young woman at the register said with a puzzled expression.

"Oh, nothing..." Merry rolled her eyes and blew out a breath. "I mean I know what I forgot now."

"Do you want to run back and get it?" The girl's words made the offer, but her face seemed to warn against it.

"No, but thanks." Merry didn't dare hold up all the shoppers waiting in line behind her, but she really needed that tape. Now she'd have to go put everything in the back of her car, return to the pandemonium in the store, find the tape, then languish in another checkout line.

"Nope," she said to herself after fighting the wind, trekking past dozens of cars to finally reach her own, and piling everything into the hatchback.

She pushed the cart to the closest cart corral, rushed back, and hopped in her car shivering. The tiny bit of warmth the sun had provided was long gone with the early setting of the sun. The tape would have to wait.

As Merry shrugged out of her coat when she got home, her daughter, Katie, poked around in the bags and asked, "Mom, did you get the tape?"

Totally exasperated and feeling guilty for not going back for what she'd forgotten, Merry grabbed the car keys out of her coat pocket and tossed them to Katie—maybe a wee bit harder than necessary.

"No, but you can go get it. Just run up to CVS or the grocery store."

Katie groaned. Any other time the seventeen-year-old would've been happy for an excuse to drive her mother's car, but not today.

"D'you know how crowded it will be up there? And it's freezing out."

"Yes, Kaitlyn Ann, I do, but the car is still warm." Like most mothers, Merry only used her children's full names in moments of utter frustration. "And if you want to wrap gifts tonight, you'd better get going. It's almost time for dinner."

Katie's only response after hearing her full name was another groan and to disappear through the entryway, slamming the door to the garage behind her.

"What's her problem?" Katie's fifteen-year-old brother asked, rooting through the stuff his mother was getting out of the bags.

"Not yours," was Merry's reply.

"Did you get tape?"

Now it was Merry's turn to groan. So maybe it *was* his problem too. "No, I forgot it, but before you get snarky, your sister is on the way to get some now."

Merry wondered what else she would do to ruin Christmas for her children when all she wanted was to make it perfect for them... in spite of everything.

"Whoa! Chill, Mom." Jimmy threw his hands up in surrender, laughed, and added, "So that's what Katie was all in a huff about." He obviously found that and anything else that bothered his sister entertaining.

"So, what do you need tape for?"

"Wrapping presents... duh, Mom."

"Careful, James!" It was never James Phillip since Philip was his father's name, and the very sound of it left a bad taste in her mouth. She didn't need to be reminded of the man who'd walked out on them and left her with two little ones to raise alone. "You don't have much to wrap, do you?"

"Nah, just a couple things." Jimmy opened the refrigerator door and gazed inside.

"What are you looking for?"

"I dunno. Something."

"Well dinner's in the crockpot, so we can eat as soon as your sister gets back."

"Okay." Jimmy grabbed a slice of cheese, wrapped it in some ham and downed it like a ravenous wolf.

Merry chuckled. She was amazed at her teen's appetite and couldn't believe how much he'd grown—and matured—over the summer. Now that his grandma wasn't around, Jimmy seemed to be taking more responsibility, and she enjoyed his boyish snarkyness now and then. He was growing up way too fast, but then they had all three had to learn their new roles in the home now that the matriarch of the family was no longer around to oversee everything.

Merry's mother, Virginia Graham—widowed when she was only forty-five—had never remarried. No one else could ever measure up to what she'd had with her Walt. So, when Merry's husband walked out on her and her two young children, Grandma had welcomed them into her home. Mrs. Graham always said her daughter and those two precious grandbabies helped fill the terrible void her Walt's death had left.

Katie and Jimmy were only five and three when their father abandoned them. Never a birthday card or a phone call—nothing. *"He was a real piece of work,"* as Grandma used to say. Merry often thought about how blessed she'd been to have known the love of a real father, and when she lost him, he'd gone to be with God, not some young red-head.

Merry's own children had to live with the knowledge that their father chose to walk out of their lives. Jimmy didn't remember him at all, and Katie only had a vague memory of the man, but they knew they had a father out there somewhere who couldn't be bothered to even send them a card at Christmas.

Grandma had done everything within her power to provide a happy home for her daughter and her grandbabies right up until she couldn't.

Pulling the last item out of the final bag, Merry stared at the new ornaments she'd purchased on an impulse—all blue and silver, her mother's favorite colors. She carried them into the family room where they would soon go on the Douglas fir Jimmy and their neighbor Fred had set up the night before.

"You'd like this one, Mom," she said admiring the tree.

"Who are you talking to?"

Merry hadn't heard her son follow her into the room. "Your grandma." She thought Jimmy might laugh at her for that, but he simply walked over and gave her a hug.

"I get that," he said before quietly leaving the room.

Your grandson is taller than I am now, Mom.

Looking at her mother's favorite rocking chair, Merry could almost see her there, her knitting basket by her side, one of her favorite shawls draped over her shoulders. She loved sitting there by the fireplace and had spent countless hours rocking little Jimmy and Katie and reading them stories right in that very spot. It was the same chair she had rocked Merry in nearly forty years before.

Merry tenderly ran her hand across the top of the antique rocker and wondered if maybe it missed her mom as much as she did. It looked so lonely sitting there empty.

2 Ash

After loading everything into the back of his BMW and shoving his cart into the helter-skelter receptacle, Asher Riggs dashed back to the car, hopped in, and was backing out of his spot when a horn blasted. He slammed on the brake, and through his rearview saw a beat-up old Chevy swerve by—but not before the driver stuck his head out of the window yelling and giving him the one-finger salute.

"And Merry Christmas to you!" Wasn't that what he thought he'd heard the woman in the store mutter under her breath?

He backed out—more cautiously this time—and as he made the turn in front of the store, stopped at the crosswalk for pedestrians. Drumming his fingers on the steering wheel, he waited as a girl, who looked to be about the same age as his daughter and unaffected by the wind blowing her open coat behind her, ambled slowly across without ever taking her eyes off her phone. He was about to proceed when a few more shoppers hurried out of the store with carts filled to overflowing, most of them rushing toward their vehicles with little or no attention to any oncoming traffic. *Trusting souls.*

Ash watched as women of every age, size, and shape hurried along, probably so they could wrap, or at least hide, all the gifts before prying eyes could see. The only other man he'd seen was the sweetheart of a guy who had saluted him moments ago. *They'll all be here on Christmas Eve.* He laughed at the thought, remembering how many Christmas Eves he'd found himself rushing around the mall looking for a few gifts for Fran, his then wife. That was when she was the only person he had to buy for. She had shopped for everyone else, and he'd taken it all for granted until he found himself on his own.

One more person, then I can finally go, he thought as a familiar looking woman, brushing her windblown hair back with one hand, pushing her cart with the other, hurried across. Recognizing her as the woman he'd run into, he hoped she wouldn't look up and see him.

She glanced in his direction, but in the closing darkness and with headlights in her eyes, Ash realized she wouldn't be able to see his face. He considered putting his window down to apologize again, but decided against it. Besides, it wasn't really his fault he'd run into her. She was the one who came to a screeching halt with no warning.

When he could finally go, he pulled out of the parking lot putting the whole silly affair out of his mind and hurried home, as much as the rush-hour and shopping traffic would allow, so he could get everything unloaded and certain items hidden before Lindsey's mother brought her home.

Ash and his ex-wife, Fran, shared custody of their seventeen-year-old daughter who spent every other week with Ash, but on the weeks she was with her father, Lindsey went to her mom's after school on Wednesdays, and Fran brought her home by eight o'clock.

Fortunately, Ash and Fran had an amicable relationship. It had hurt like crazy when she left him because—as she said—his work at the hospital took so much time away from her and the family. Dr. Asher Riggs had tried everything to save his marriage, even leaving the demanding schedule of the hospital to work in a practice where he'd have more regular hours. Unfortunately, by then Fran had already moved too far away emotionally and found solace in the arms of someone new, and that someone had soon become Lindsey's stepfather.

Ash struggled with that at times, but at least it seemed Fran never spoke badly of him, nor did he of her. They were determined not to hurt their daughter any more than their separation and divorce may have already.

This would be Ash's third Christmas since the divorce, and he wouldn't have his daughter with him on Christmas day, but they would observe the holiday when Lindsey was with him on Christmas Eve.

He knew their time together was nothing like the big gathering at her mother's, but it was always a perfect day to them. They had developed their own special traditions. They would head to the IHOP across town for a big Christmas breakfast, then come back and open gifts before going to his parents' home in the neighborhood where he'd grown up for a beautiful spread of ham, turkey, meatballs, potato salad, cheese board and all the things that completed their Christmas feast, and of course, more presents. The Riggs were extremely generous with their only grandchild as well as their son, so later in the day, after a fun filled afternoon, he would load up the car to take all their goodies home—but not before one more important stop.

As soon as he got back to his home on Cherryhill Lane, Ash got busy hiding the few of his most recent purchases for his daughter. His walk-in closet already contained an assortment of mostly wrapped boxes—thanks to Lindsey's mother clueing him in to some things she wanted and her correct sizes—so he added these to the pile and just in time.

"Dad, I'm home!"

Ash got a kick out of how his daughter chased away the silence that filled the house when she wasn't there.

"Be right there, Linds!" he called back. He covered everything up with an old blanket, pulled the door closed, and turned to find a grinning Lindsey standing in his doorway.

"Whatcha doin', Pops?" She plopped down on her father's bed next to all the bags he had dropped there before rushing her gifts into the closet. Wearing a devilish smile, Lindsey asked, "What's in the bags?"

"Nothing for you, my dear." He gathered up several of the sacks and headed out of his bedroom with his daughter right on his heels. "But I wouldn't mind a bit if you want to grab some and help me wrap them."

"Oh, is it more stuff for the old folks?" Lindsey scoffed but went back and picked up the remaining bags and followed her father down the hall toward the kitchen.

"Yeah, most of it. You want to get me the scissors and tape, please?"

Ash emptied the contents of the first bag onto the huge island next to the wrapping paper he'd dropped there earlier on his way through. This kitchen, the whole house for that matter, was much bigger than Ash needed, but it was the home Lindsey had grown up in, and he stayed in it more for her than for himself.

"Not to be mean, but do they like even know it's Christmas?"

"Lindsey! C'mon, you know better. Lots of the residents, most of them really, are as lucid as you and I."

"Well, yeah, but not all of them. I mean like I've seen some of them just sit and rock or stare out the window."

"I know, but even those patients are sometimes more aware of what's going on than you realize, and a little kindness may mean more to them than they can show." Ash handed Lindsey the gift he had finished wrapping. "Could you help me write the tags? This one is for Happy Jack."

Lindsey stuck the tag and a small ribbon on the package. "So is Happy Jack going to be happy with getting socks for Christmas?" She wrinkled her nose at the thought.

"Yes, his poor feet are always cold, and he'll love these warm socks. Besides, there's a reason he's called 'Happy' Jack. There's a lot that other people could learn from his positive attitude, and he does so much to pick up the spirits of other patients when they're having a bad day."

"Well, don't get me socks for Christmas, okay?" she said, patting her dad on the top of his head then plopping onto the bar stool across from him, resting her chin on her hands.

Ash laughed at his daughter's antics and pulled a white pashmina out of a bag. "I'm going to need one of those small boxes for this one."

"Oh wow, this is so soft… lots better than socks." Lindsey laid a piece of red tissue paper in the bottom of a box before folding and putting the scarf in it. "Who is this one for?"

"That's for a very special lady, Miss Ginny. You may remember her. She often stares out over the meadow, but she loves soft things, and sometimes responds to the sense of touch. When she does, her eyes come alive. I think Miss Ginny must have been a beautiful woman when she was younger. Or maybe it is the wit and wisdom she has gained with age that made her a beautiful person."

3 MERRY

Thursday, December 19

Merry held the camel's head in one hand and its body in the other, both wet with tears. She had worried Jimmy or Katie might break one of the precious treasures, but it was she who sat with the broken pieces in her hands.

With less than a week until Christmas, Merry had been busy decorating, trying to make the house as festive as years past—with all the joy and beauty her mother had always created—but with tears of frustration rolling down her cheeks, she felt no joy.

The five-foot fir stood at the front window waiting to be adorned by Katie and Jimmy this weekend. Since tomorrow would be their last day of school until after New Year's, they'd have plenty of time but would probably be of little help with all the myriad of other things that had to be done, but that was okay. That's not what had started the waterworks flowing.

Mrs. Graham had made the nativity set in her ceramics class more than twenty years ago, and every year Merry would watch as her mother tenderly unwrapped each individual piece and placed them on the lace covering of the beautiful mahogany drum table between the two wingback chairs in the living room. Then Mrs. Graham would sigh and declare, *"Now we can decorate the tree."*

Merry wondered for a moment what her mother would say if she was there. Would she be distraught? *I'm sorry, Mom.* Then, glancing at the empty rocking chair in front of the fireplace, she could almost see her mother's face and she knew exactly what she'd say.

Superglue!

Merry spent the next twenty minutes searching the house for said Superglue but to no avail. She had a million other things to do—at least that's how it felt—but she could focus on only one thing. Superglue!

Giving up on finding it, she finally grabbed her keys and coat and made a beeline for the closest place to buy some, at CVS.

She was in luck. Although it took a lot longer than she had hoped—seems everybody was there needing some last-minute item or another—she finally got back home and made the necessary repair. With another silent apology to her mother, Merry finished setting up the display and thought, *Now we can decorate the Christmas tree.*

Except, that would have to wait. Merry had other priorities as she moved on to the next item on her list—cookies.

There had to be cookies, and she wanted them to be as delicious as the ones her mother had baked every year. Well, every year until last Christmas when her dementia had begun to steal her away. Grandma knew what all the ingredients were, but she had needed help with things like setting the temperature on the oven and remembering she was baking cookies at all. One batch of peanut butter cookies would have burned to a crisp if Merry hadn't heard the timer and come to their rescue. Merry had found Grandma sitting in her rocking chair by the fire knitting a prayer shawl. She had forgotten all about them, and rather than upset her mother, Merry had quietly taken them out of the oven and put the final cookie sheet in.

Merry opened the file box and found her mom's recipe card for the snickerdoodles. They were the kids' favorite, and she was determined to make them as good as her mother's. Hers were always soft and chewy, a melt in your mouth delight.

"Here goes, Mom. Wish me luck." As soon as she'd uttered the words, she could imagine her mother's response.

"It's not about luck, dear. Just follow my recipe. It's all right there for you."

First, she put the butter and sugar in her mom's big mixing bowl and creamed them. She could hear her mother saying, *"Remember you have to do it for four or five minutes so the butter will coat the sugar crystals."*

Merry watched for the perfect texture. When it looked light and fluffy, just like her mom's had, she added the eggs and vanilla and creamed them some more.

Grateful her mother had written down the recipe years ago, Merry double-checked the amounts then stirred in the flour, cream of tartar, baking soda, and salt. Since her mother had always popped the dough into the refrigerator for at least fifteen minutes, Merry mixed up the cinnamon and sugar then made herself a sandwich while she waited for the dough to chill.

After she wolfed down her sandwich, she got the dough out and rolled it into small balls. She had only been about five years old when her mother first let her do this task and roll them around in the sugar and cinnamon. *How am I doing, Mom?*

After getting the first batch in the oven, Merry ran out to get the mail which was mostly ads, a few bills, and lots of Christmas cards. Half a dozen of them were addressed to her mother. She sighed and set them to the side.

One card in a green envelope caught her attention. It was addressed to "The Snyders" in a familiar hand. *Aunt Carolyn!* Merry ran to the secretary to get one of the few family cards she had left. *How could I forget Aunt Carolyn?* She quickly scribbled a brief message under the picture of her, Katie, Jimmy, and her mom—a picture taken over the summer—and addressed the envelope. She was about to put a stamp on the envelope when she smelled it.

"No!" She sprinted to the kitchen and yanked the oven door open. Too late. No one wanted black snickerdoodles. The last straw was when the smoke alarm screamed.

Merry screamed back.

She slammed the oven door, fanned the smoke detector with a dish towel, then opened the kitchen slider to clear out the smoke that had filled the room. Totally spent, she sat on the floor and wept.

"All right. Shake it off." Merry wiped her face with the dishtowel she was still holding, dragged herself up off the kitchen floor, and with a huge sigh, put the second batch of snickerdoodles in the oven.

She spent the rest of the afternoon making dozens of snickerdoodles, chocolate chip, and sugar cookies—ever watchful so as not to burn them—and putting them in tins when they cooled (after sampling one from each batch), but there was also a plate of decorated sugar cookies on the kitchen table when Katie and Jimmy got home from school.

The last batch had come out of the oven moments before, so they were still soft and warm, and the aroma of Christmas brought the teens bounding into the kitchen, tossing their bags aside and diving into them.

"Oh wow, these are so good!" Jimmy said through a mouthful of cookie. "They taste just like Grandma's."

Katie—always the serious, sensitive child—wrapped her arms around her mom whose eyes had filled with tears. "Jimmy!" she scolded.

"No, honey, it's okay. That's what I was going for, you know." Merry smiled through a blur of tears she refused to let fall. This first Christmas without Grandma bustling around the house was going to be hard, but they would get through it.

"Sorry, Mom," Jimmy said.

"No, seriously sweetie, that's the nicest thing you could have said."

Jimmy grabbed two more cookies off the plate.

"Okay, that's enough now. It's almost dinner time."

"What are we having?" Katie asked.

Merry had been so focused on Christmas cookies, she hadn't even thought about what to fix for dinner, and since she had promised to be at the church by seven o'clock to help wrap presents for their "angel families," there was no time to waste.

"How about pizza?"

Cheers from two teenagers provided their approval, and though Merry chastised herself for not planning a more nutritious meal, she knew she could never go wrong with Papa John's.

4 ASH

"Too often we underestimate the power of a touch, a smile, a kind word, a listening ear, an honest compliment, or the smallest act of caring, all of which have the potential to turn a life around."
—Leo Buscaglia

Friday, December 20

Every Friday, Dr. Riggs spent the entire day at Vigilant Care, and it was his favorite day of the week. After nearly fifteen years at Mercy Hospital where he thought he'd been satisfied with his choice, he'd changed direction and found his true fit, his real passion.

Ash had made the change so he'd have more time to spend with his family and to possibly save his failing marriage, and although it hadn't done that, it had shown him where his heart was—geriatrics.

It may have been, at least in part, because of the special bond between Ash and his grandfather and what he'd witnessed as the elderly man slowly declined until he seemed to fade away to nothing. Ash hadn't really understood at the time, but he remembered the old man sitting in his rocking chair in the corner of the living room, left out and seemingly oblivious to everything going on around him.

The only time Grandpa Eugene smiled and seemed to come to life was when six-year-old Asher climbed on his lap with a book in his hand, and said, "Read to me, Gramps." Then the old man would become animated as he read, pointing to each word for Ash to follow along. Sometimes he would even tickle his young grandson and echo the child's giggles.

By the time Ash was ten, the rocking chair was empty.

All these years later, Ash would sometimes look into one of his elderly patient's eyes and recognize that same look. Then he would do everything within his power to reach that person and draw them out. Bringing them back was his super power and his greatest joy.

"Good morning, Miss Tilly. How are you on this fine day?" Ash usually began his rounds with ninety-six-year-old Matilda Martin, and he was almost always greeted by her sweet smile and enthusiastic, though shaky, voice repeating the same refrain.

But this morning he didn't see her usual smile. There was no "Good morning." She wasn't even out of bed, which was unusual for her. Miss Tilly was typically up, dressed, and sitting by the window reading her devotionals by the time he checked in on her.

Ash circled the bed and took a seat in the nearby chair, pulling it closer and observing his patient carefully. She was staring down at her hands, and when the doctor placed one of his own over hers, she slowly raised her gaze to look at him.

"I'm so old," she said weakly. "Do you know I'll be ninety-seven on Monday? Ninety-seven!"

"Yes, I know, but you are the youngest ninety-six-year-old I've ever known... and I bet you'll be the youngest ninety-seven-year-old, too." As he patted her hand, he watched the corners of her mouth curve up into a dubious smile. Encouraging, but not the sunshiny one he was used to.

Stethoscope in hand, he said, "Let's have a listen, okay?"

Checking her vitals, he found everything was good. With her medication, Miss Tilly's blood pressure was within an acceptable range, her pulse was strong and steady, and there was no fever. Physically, there was no change from the last time he'd seen her. He checked the chart and found nothing unusual or alarming except one notation.

The patient is experiencing a loss of appetite and demonstrates a loss of interest in participating in daily recreational activities. Displays signs of depression.

After completing his examination and spending a bit more time with his first patient than usual, Ash moved to the person in the next room and continued his rounds, but his concern for Miss Tilly followed him throughout the rest of the morning.

It was nearing lunchtime when he returned to her room and discovered Tilly was out of bed but still not dressed. She looked lost and alone sitting by the window—not reading—just staring out across the meadow at the row of barren trees standing unadorned with no hint of their future cherry blossomed beauty. Her mood seemed as gray as the dismal December sky.

Ash couldn't make the sun come out in the sky, but he was determined to bring back her sunny smile.

"Well now, Miss Tilly..."

The old lady jumped at the sound of his voice.

"Sorry, I didn't mean to startle you, but how am I supposed to take you to lunch in your dressing gown? I mean it's all right with me of course, but don't you usually dress before going to the dining room?"

Tilly looked baffled. "I... I thought I'd take lunch in my room today. I don't really feel much like going down to the dining hall."

"Hmm, so you're turning down my invitation? I'm hurt." Ash's devilish grin seemed to soften his patient's resolve.

"You mean you're going to have lunch with me? In the dining hall?"

"Well, that was the plan... but if you'd rather not—"

"No, no, that would be lovely." This time her smile was beaming. "I'll just need a few minutes to dress, dear."

"There's no rush, Miss Tilly. Take it slow. I have some phone calls to make, and there's plenty of time." Ash checked his watch. "It's only eleven-thirty. I'll be back to accompany you to lunch in about twenty-five minutes, m'lady." His big grin and bow brought a bit of a giggle out of Matilda. At last Ash was getting a glimpse of the Miss Tilly he was used to seeing. Now he had only to figure out how to keep her from drifting back into that malaise.

A little before noon, with her walking cane in one hand and her other hand resting on her doctor's arm, Matilda Martin walked down the long hall to lunch with her date.

Ash guided her to one of the large, still empty round tables.

"Look who's here. It's Doctor R. What's the occasion, Doc?" Happy Jack's sonorous voice rang out. Without waiting for an answer, he called across the room. "Hey Gladys, over here."

Within moments, all eight seats at the table were occupied and filled with animated conversation and laughter. Happy Jack kept the energy level high, and Ash was pleased to see his date joining in the conversation with all the other nonagenarians. More importantly, amid all the chatter, Tilly was eating.

He smiled, thinking he'd found the right medicine for his patient, at least for the short-term, but he wondered if it was enough.

5 Merry

"Blessed is the season which engages the whole world in a conspiracy of love."
—Hamilton Wright Mabie

There were times when working from home got lonely. The benefits by far outweighed any negative aspects of her new situation, but Merry sometimes missed the interaction she used to have with her coworkers.

It was different when her mother had been busily preparing something in the kitchen, puttering around the house, or watching one of her shows, but now that she was gone, the house was too quiet. Even when Virginia Graham had begun declining, she would sit in her rocking chair for hours doing her counted cross stitch, knitting, or crocheting prayer shawls while humming a tune. *Oh Mom, I miss you so much.*

Merry knew the awful stillness would disappear when Katie and Jimmy came barreling in the door after school, but that was hours away. The article she was editing was tedious, and the monastic silence deafening.

"Alexa, play music for relaxation."

The device switched on and that helped for a while, but despite the four cups of coffee she'd downed over the last few hours, Merry found herself getting drowsy. After double-checking her schedule to make sure she had no Zoom or conference calls the rest of the afternoon, she pushed her chair back from the desk, stretched, and headed for the kitchen to refill her cup.

"Oh crap!" Seeing the empty basket killed that idea. She'd used the last of the Truvia, and drinking her coffee without sweetener was out of the question. "Now what?"

Merry answered her own question by pulling her coat out of the closet and grabbing her keys off the hook on her way to the garage. She would go to the store for sweetener and a few other things she'd added to her list since the last trip, but first, a quick stop at Latte Da for a change of pace.

As she backed the car out of the garage, Fred, her next-door neighbor waved her down. He and his wife, Judy, were good friends and had been there to help Mrs. Graham ever since she lost her husband all those years ago. Now Fred was there for Merry and her children.

Merry put the window down. "Hey Fred, what's up?"

"I still have about another hour's worth of work to finish up the basement and get 'er done. D'ya want me to get on it now before the kids come home and catch me?"

"Absolutely! Do you have your key with you?"

Fred pulled his loaded keychain out of his pocket and jingled it in the air. "Got it."

"Thanks, Fred. You're a Godsend, and they're going to love it." Merry put the car in gear and backed onto the street smiling. This was going to be a great Christmas for the kids. *Unless I mess it up.* But her smile faded when she thought of her mother and how much she would have loved seeing the surprise and delight on her grandchildren's faces.

Determined not to let her melancholy mood ruin the holiday for Katie and Jimmy, she pushed the sadness aside and focused on treating herself and lifting her mood when she got to her favorite coffee shop.

The familiar and comforting aroma of coffee greeted her like a warm hug when she entered.

"Hi, Bobby. I'll do the usual cappuccino and blueberry scone, please." She hadn't needed to look at the board to know what she wanted. This was her special treat and standard order whenever she stopped at Latte Da.

"Sure thing," Bobby the barista said as he slipped the tongs around a freshly made scone. "That's for here, right, Merry?"

Making sure she wasn't changing her typical routine, he put the English delight on a plate and passed it across the counter. "That's $6.75."

Before she could tap her credit card, a man's hand reached in front of her.

"I've got this," he said.

Stunned, Merry looked up into the eyes of a man she only knew as "the jerkface."

"But—"

"I doubt if you remember me, but I'd like to make up for the other day. I'm the guy that ran into you with my shopping cart. So... if you don't mind."

"I, um... that really isn't necessary."

"Please? I don't want to leave you with the impression I'm a real jerk." He winked when he said it.

Maybe he did hear me. Merry quickly looked away.

"I was in a rush to finish up and get home so I could hide some things before my daughter got there. I should have apologized for running into you then."

She hadn't noticed those puppy dog eyes when they'd been at the store, or the dimple when he smiled. But then there hadn't been any smiling at the time. Now she was mortified by the possibility that he'd heard her silly comment.

"Well, thank you. That's very nice of you." She looked up and their eyes met and held briefly before she turned away. Maybe he wasn't such a jerk after all. The frustration of trying to get everything done and make Christmas perfect tended to make everyone a bit cranky. She ought to know. Merry smiled at Bobby who'd been waiting patiently during the exchange.

"What are you having, Ash? The usual?" Bobby asked the man with the dimple.

Feeling the heat in her cheeks, Merry took her scone to a small table near the window where she could enjoy the warmth of the sun without the wind that would greet her when she walked out the coffee shop door.

"Here you go." It wasn't Bobby or the girl working with him this morning who placed the steaming hot cappuccino on the table. It was the jerk, aka the man with the dimple, aka Ash. "It's Merry, right?"

"Yes... and thanks again." Merry pushed the ever-dangling strands of hair behind her ear and remembered she hadn't bothered with a lick of makeup. She had gotten rather careless about that since working from home.

"You're welcome. Have a nice day, Merry."

Merry sighed as he went out the door and realized she was slightly disappointed that he'd gotten his order to go. She watched him dash across the street and noticed how the wind blew his dark brown hair and how he ran his fingers through it after getting into his shiny, raspberry red BMW. *Nice...*

Merry took a long sip of her cappuccino and sighed. *And here I am looking like heaven knows what. But...*

As she watched the BMW pull away from the curb, there was something about the whole image that made her uneasy. Then a sudden flashback made it all clear. On another windy, December day, she had watched her ex—the deserter—throw the last of his belongings into a similar vehicle, a much older model, of course. It was twelve years ago, after all, but yes, a red BMW.

Men and their fancy cars, who needs 'em? Not me!

6 Ash

"Once again, we come to the Holiday Season, a deeply religious time that each of us observes, in his own way, by going to the mall of his choice."

—Dave Barry

Saturday, December 21

It was nearly ten-thirty when Lindsey finally drifted into the kitchen where Ash sat sipping coffee and working on his laptop in his usual morning spot at the over-sized island.

"Good morning, sunshine." He drained his coffee mug and couldn't resist teasing his favorite girl who didn't appear quite ready to shine. But after all, Saturdays were meant for sleeping in, at least for some people. Ash had been up since five-thirty himself.

"Morning." Lindsey moseyed over to the Keurig and popped a French-vanilla cappuccino in to brew. "Mmm, what have you got there, Daddy dearest?"

"Did you want one of these? Oops, sorry. This was the last one." Seeing his daughter's smile fade and her shoulders slump, he quickly relented. "Just kidding. Open your sleepy eyes and look around."

Ash laughed when she finally spied and pounced on the box of cinnamon buns on the other end of the counter.

Lindsey had inherited her father's sweet tooth. She took a big bite before adding two teaspoons of sugar to her coffee and coming to sit next to her dad.

"One of these days, all that sugar's going to catch up with you. Then you're gonna have to work out like I do every morning."

"You know you don't really have to."

"I do if I want to keep my boyish figure."

"You look great, Dad... I mean like for an old guy."

"Hey! I'm not that old, kid," Ash said before returning his attention to his notes on the computer screen.

"Yeah, I know, but you're like not getting any younger, you know."

Ash snickered, gave his daughter the side-eye, and returned his attention to his work.

"Do you have to do that now?" Lindsey asked with a mouthful of cinnamon bun. She leaned her head on his shoulder. "You're always working."

She's right. Ash was devoted to his work—which contributed to the demise of his marriage—but after his wife left him, he had made it his whole life. It was what had kept him going after his personal life had fallen apart.

"Da-ad!"

Ash heard the impatience in Lindsey's voice. *What am I doing?* Fighting his urge to complete the paperwork, he firmly closed the laptop and turned to his daughter.

"Okay, kiddo. I'm all yours. What do you want to talk about?"

Lindsey beamed. "I'm hungry. How 'bout some waffles?"

"You're always hungry," Ash teased, but he couldn't help but envy how she could eat anything without gaining a pound.

When he pushed his chair back, Lindsey jumped up with a sudden burst of energy and told him to stay put. He often wondered how so much energy could be packed into such a petite package.

"I'll do it." She retrieved the waffle iron from the huge walk-in pantry and started pulling out the ingredients. Ash watched in fascination as she got out the eggs, flour, sugar, milk, and butter. "Do you have any vanilla extract?" She wrinkled her nose at his negative response, then added, "No worries, it's good without... just better with."

Seeing his "little girl" busily preparing their breakfast, he was struck by how much she had grown up when he wasn't looking.

He was so lost in thought, he wasn't really listening to Lindsey's steady flow of chatter until she turned to look at him with her hands on her hips.

"Hello? Where did you go?"

"I'm sorry, I was watching my grownup little girl. What did you say?"

"You're funny. I asked when you're gonna start dating again. Like I keep saying, you're not getting any younger." She poured the batter, closed the waffle iron, and turned back waiting for an answer. "Just cuz the last time was like a disaster doesn't mean you should give up. It's been like a year since you even went out."

Ash remembered the woman he had gone out with nearly a year ago. Barbara was attractive enough, but all she wanted to do was go to clubs, and that wasn't his scene. Twenty years earlier he'd enjoyed occasionally "letting his hair down" at the bar scene, but then he got married and had a kid. Everything changed after that.

"I don't have the time nor the desire for dating." Funny thing how at that moment a certain brunette with messy hair and deep, dark, seductive brown eyes popped into his mind.

"I do."

"What?" Ash's head jutted forward, and his eyes grew wide. "Excuse me?"

"Don't get all crazy, Dad. It's not like a big deal... but Thursday, this guy in debate club asked me if I wanna catch a movie sometime over Christmas break."

Ash tried to compose himself. Lindsey had never talked about wanting to date, but he knew this day was bound to come. Although his little girl would soon be eighteen, she had always put all her energy into academics, debate club, and her voice and guitar lessons. He swallowed hard, realizing he was looking at a truly lovely young woman... but she was still his little girl.

"So what's this guy's name, and what does your mother think of all this?"

"Elliot, and I didn't tell her about him yet. Rodney was around all the time Thursday night, and I didn't need to hear his opinion." Lindsey rolled her eyes and set the maple syrup and a perfectly cooked waffle in front of her father. "Besides, I'm here with you this week, so they don't even need to know."

"Oh, I'm not so sure about that." Ash felt a certain satisfaction that he was the first to know and his daughter hadn't felt comfortable talking about it with her stepfather, Rodney.

"Whatever. I'll tell Mom about it when I go over Wednesday." Lindsey poured a generous amount of syrup on her waffle. "Wow, I can't believe Christmas is this close."

"Yeah, but let's not change the subject. When were you planning on going to this movie?"

"Monday." Lindsey snickered. "Elliot just got his license and doesn't have a car yet, so I said I could meet him there. It's not that far to walk... or you could drive me..."

"Oh, I see. You butter me up by making my favorite breakfast so I'll take you to meet this guy." Ash saw his daughter's look of total indignation.

"That's not true," she said emphatically. Her expression quickly turned into a sullen pout.

"I'm kidding, Linds. Of course, I'll drive you. Now tell me more about this loser you're going out with."

He winked to make sure she knew he was still joking then listened as she gushed about how clever Elliot was and how he was already planning to apply to Harvard and study law. She didn't say a word about what he looked like.

"So does he have a big wart on his nose or something?"

"What?" Lindsey looked baffled.

"I'm wondering why you haven't said a thing about what he looks like."

"Oh... well, he's like gorgeous, of course," Lindsey said with a sly grin.

Hmm, gorgeous, he thought to himself. *Like, what was her name? Merry... yeah, Merry.*

"So what do you want to do for lunch, Pops?"

"You can't possibly be thinking about lunch when you haven't even finished your breakfast."

Ash watched as his daughter popped the last big bite of waffle in her mouth, used her napkin to catch the syrup dripping down her chin, and said something unintelligible.

"What?" He had to laugh at her attempt to speak through the mouthful of food.

"I said it's almost lunchtime."

"You're such a squirrel," Ash said tousling his daughter's hair on his way to put his dish in the dishwasher. "I think we just had brunch."

"Okay, I guess. Then what do you want to do today?" Lindsey said, absently picking up her phone and starting to scroll.

"Maybe if you put your phone away and get dressed, I'll let you decide. We can go visit Grammy and Pap, or hang out and watch a movie."

"I've got a better idea. You can take me to the mall. I still have to finish my Christmas shopping."

"The weekend before Christmas? D'you have any idea how crowded the stores will be today?"

"Sure, I don't care." Lindsey grinned. "It's fun."

"If you say so." He could already imagine how crazy the traffic would be around the mall. He didn't consider that fun himself, but he had told his "little girl" she could pick.

"All right, we'll do the mall thing, and if you don't take all day, maybe we'll stop and you can get something at Latte Da on the way back."

"Yay!" Lindsey jumped from her spot and dashed off to her room, leaving her empty plate without a thought to cleaning up after herself.

Normally Ash would have called her back, reminding her she'd forgotten something, but he chose to let it go this time. He wanted to get this trip into the chaos of last-minute shoppers over with. He was already looking forward to the stop they'd make on the way home. You never know who you might run into at Latte Da.

***

Ash had not underestimated the mall madness they'd encounter, but it was obviously a successful trip for his daughter. As Dad, he had been assigned some bench warming time when Lindsey got to a couple of stores and said he wasn't allowed to go in with her. But he enjoyed people-watching, and it was all worth it when he saw the delight on his daughter's face as she emerged victorious and exclaimed that she was done.

Using an extra dose of patience, Ash crawled through the traffic and was relieved when they got away from the busy shopping area and pulled into the small parking lot next to his favorite coffee shop. At least it wasn't crowded at three in the afternoon, and he didn't have to find a spot on the street.

Following his daughter inside, he scanned the few occupied tables. Unfortunately, there was no one he recognized—no one with adorable wind-blown hair and gorgeous brown eyes.

7 MERRY

"The earth has grown old with its burden of care, but at Christmas it always is young, the heart of the jewel burns lustrous and fair, and its soul full of music breaks the air, when the song of angels is sung."
—Phillips Brooks

Sunday, December 22

Merry slipped the emerald green dress over her head and stepped into her two-inch pumps. She rarely ever wore either anymore, and she hadn't been to church even once since her mother wasn't around to remind her to hurry so they wouldn't be late.

"Oh darling," her mom would say. *"Why don't you wear your pretty green dress this morning? It's so much more flattering than those pants outfits."*

"That may be, Mom, but this is a lot more comfortable... and warmer. Besides, you don't want to be late."

"I know, but if you hurry... and you have such nice legs. You should flaunt them while you can."

Merry smiled at the thought. She couldn't remember a single occasion when she had listened to her mother and changed into one of the few dresses she still had hanging in her closet. She glanced in the mirror and had to concede that her mother was right. Her long legs were accentuated by the shoes she'd chosen.

"This is for you, Mom," she whispered. *Certainly not for anyone else.*

Merry looked in the mirror again and had an idea. She went into her mother's old room—which was exactly as she had left it—

opened the jewelry box, and lifted out the opal necklace and earrings. Opal was her mother's birthstone, and Merry had saved like crazy and gifted her this set fifteen years ago for her sixtieth birthday.

While corralling her then two-year-old Katie who was running around Grandma's living room and bouncing newborn Jimmy in her arms, Merry had only had a moment to accept her mother's hug, but she remembered how the older woman had brushed away the tears before offering to hold little Jimmy.

"You certainly have your hands full with these two."

"You can say that again," Merry had replied.

"Where's Phil? Why didn't he come along today?"

"He had to work again."

"On Saturday? I never knew a dentist to have to work so many Saturdays."

"I know, but he got a call this morning and said some woman was in pain and needed an emergency visit." Merry had some doubts about what kind of service this so-called patient really needed, but she had no idea that a few years later he would walk out and she'd be the one left in pain to raise her young children alone.

Merry shook the thought from her mind. Looking back at the lovely opals, she quickly put them on.

"Mom, we're gonna be late!"

Merry was struck by how much Katie's voice sounded like Virginia Graham, but in a flash, she was answering. "I'm ready," she said. "Jimmy, are you coming?"

Jimmy answered by walking out of his bedroom, still in his pajamas, with his disheveled hair and half-opened eyes. "Yeah... I don't think so." He grinned then added, "I gotta eat breakfast. 'Sides, I'm not dressed for the occasion."

"Okay, sleepyhead." Merry gave him a quick kiss on the cheek and tousled his hair.

"Bye, goofball," Katie said. Then turning to her mom she asked, "Can I drive?"

Katie got them safely to the church on time—she always drove with extra care when her mother was in the car—and they headed for a pew toward the front out of habit. Merry had always liked to sit where she had a good view of her mother in the choir. Even when dementia had taken that away from them, Virginia Graham had continued to attend services and sing the familiar hymns. They were like a magic elixir that brought light into her eyes.

The sanctuary looked magnificent this morning. Two giant evergreen trees decorated with white lights stood on either side of the altar. Pine roping draped down the sides of the pews and arced from window to window. Masses of poinsettias sat on either side of the steps leading to the altar and the beautiful advent candle waiting for its fourth candle to be lit.

"Grandma would've loved how pretty everything is," Katie whispered.

Merry squeezed her daughter's hand the way she knew her mother would have done hers, and she had to blink back the tears that threatened to fall. The battle against them continued throughout the service as they sang the familiar carols.

The service began with "Oh Come All Ye Faithful" and ended with "Joy to the World," but it was the hymn right before the sermon that constricted Merry's throat.

"This was Grandma's favorite," Katie said as they opened their hymnals to "O Holy Night."

With a quick glance through the blur of her own tears, Merry saw her daughter's chin quivering. She plucked a tissue from her purse and handed it to Katie whose face so reminded her of pictures of her mother at about that age. The same curly blonde hair and bright blue eyes as the young Virginia Graham whose hair had slowly turned to the color of snow, but whose eyes were forever the color of the sea.

Though her throat had grown tight, Merry pulled herself together and gave the song all she had—except for those really high notes where she was forced to lip-sync—like she was singing with her momma once again... as she had every Christmas since she could remember.

Fortunately, by the final notes of "Joy to the World" her spirits were lifted—at least for the moment—and as they were filing out of the church, she could see the joy reflected on most of the other parishioners' faces, including one face she hadn't expected to see.

Merry hesitated a moment trying to remember his name. Then she recalled what Bobby the barista had called him. *Ash.*

"Mom, what's wrong? Why'd you stop?" Katie, who had been walking behind and slightly to the left of her mother, put her hand out to keep from running into her.

"Sorry, I saw someone I thought I knew."

"Where? Who is it?"

"Nobody, really. Just the man over there with the young girl."

"Oh, he's hot," Katie said as they neared the narthex and Ash and his daughter exited.

"Katie! You're in church."

This time she spoke in a whisper and followed her words with a snicker. "Yeah well, that doesn't make him less hot."

Once outside, Katie was the one who stopped when she looked at her mother's face.

"Oh my gosh... you're blushing!" This time she laughed right out loud.

"I am not. Don't be ridiculous."

"Yeah, right. I guess you think he's hot too." Katie charged ahead, blonde ponytail swinging madly. "I'm driving!"

Merry tried to keep her eyes on Katie who was dashing to the driver's side of the car, but she couldn't resist another peek in the direction Ash had taken, and there it was. That gorgeous raspberry red BMW. And the guy getting in it wasn't half bad either, she had to admit. The only person she could see with him was the girl who looked about the same age as her daughter. *So, if he's married, where's his wife?*

She didn't realize she was staring until the familiar stranger saw her and raised his hand in a wave.

Oh no... Not knowing what else to do, she lifted her hand to shoulder height then hurried to get in the passenger side of her own car.

"Okay, give." Katie was wearing a sly and somewhat annoying I-know-what's-going-on smile.

All Merry would give her was a side-eye and, "Just drive." How could she answer her daughter's question when she had no idea what was going on herself? Why did seeing this stranger make her heart beat faster?

Shake it off, Merry. Long ago she had decided she didn't need a man in her life. After being dumped by a high school sweetheart who had broken her heart and a husband who'd walked out on them, she knew all she needed to know about men. *I don't need them, and they can't be trusted.*

But one thing she had to admit. Katie was right... this Ash guy was hot.

8 ASH

"Who was that?" Lindsey asked.

"Who?"

"The woman you waved to."

"Oh, nobody." Ash looked straight ahead as he pulled out of the church parking lot, but he could feel his daughter staring at him, and when he finally glanced her way, he knew she wasn't going to let up.

He couldn't stop the grin that had been threatening ever since he saw the woman looking his way. She looked a lot more put together than the last time he'd seen her—even more stunning.

"All right, Dad. Give. The way you're grinning, you can't tell me she's nobody. Have you been holding out on me?"

"No, I'm not kidding. I don't even really know her. She's just a woman I ran into." Ash chuckled, remembering that first encounter. He'd been in a rather bad mood and couldn't believe how this crazy woman had stopped in the middle of the aisle. But now he was glad she had, otherwise he may never have met her... and somehow that was unthinkable.

"I'm waiting," Lindsey said. "Tell me. Look at your face. You like her, don't you?"

Unable to escape his daughter's challenging stare, Ash gave in and told her all about the store incident and how he'd tried to apologize by means of paying for her order at Latte Da.

"So, like I said, you like her." She sang like Sandra Bullock in *Miss Congeniality*. "You like her, you want to date her."

Ash couldn't help but laugh with her but had to set her straight. "Listen, Linds. Yes, she's attractive, but how can I *like* the woman when I don't know anything about her? She could be an absolute shrew. Besides, it looks like she has a daughter, so she's probably married."

"You have a daughter," Lindsey scoffed. "You're not married… maybe she's not either."

Ash thought it was ridiculous to pursue this line of thinking about a total stranger, but he hoped his daughter was right. Plus he was certain she was far from being a shrew. *And we go to the same church.* Though he had fallen into the habit of only going to church on the Sundays when Lindsey was with him, he thought he should probably start showing up more regularly.

He had begun attending St. Matthews nearly a year ago when he got tired of seeing his ex with her new husband at St. Josephs. Their divorce may have been amicable, but he didn't really need to see the "happy couple" every week, especially when Lindsey was with them, and he was sitting all alone.

He imagined how nice it would be to once again sit with someone—a very specific someone—with their daughters sitting between them as they worshipped together.

"Do you know what's for dinner?" Lindsey's voice snapped him out of his frivolous daydream.

"What?" Ash said.

"Do you know what Grammy is having for dinner today? I'm starving!"

"No idea, but we're almost there so you can ask her yourself, and be sure you offer to help."

Instead of having his parents come to dinner every other Sunday as he and Fran had, Sunday dinner at his parents' home had become a weekly tradition since his divorce, but sometimes he worried his mom might get tired of cooking a big meal for them every week.

"I always do, and she always finds something for me to do, but I think she really likes doing it herself."

The delicious aroma of a turkey dinner greeted them when they entered through the garage and straight into the kitchen.

"Mmm, that smells so yummy, Grammy. Smells like Thanksgiving."

"Well, since your mother always has a ham on Christmas day, I thought we'd have turkey today. Besides, since you weren't here for Thanksgiving, I thought you might enjoy having some of my stuffing and gravy."

After giving her granddaughter a big bearhug, Mrs. Riggs hugged her son and asked him to get the turkey out of the oven before going to join his father in the living room. "And tell your dad he can start carving in about fifteen minutes."

"What can I do, Grammy?" Lindsey asked.

"I've got everything under control here, but you can finish setting the table if you'd like."

Ash watched his mother bustling around the kitchen and was reminded of what a young seventy-one-year-old she was. It put his mind at ease that she showed no signs of the dementia her father had suffered.

Ash got out of the way—the kitchen in his old family home was a little small for three or more people—and joined his father who had been watching an old movie from behind his eyelids.

Albert Riggs's eyes popped open at the sound of his son's chuckle.

"You look pretty comfy there, Dad. Stay put," Ash said as his father started to get up. "You've got about fifteen minutes before Mom needs you to carve the bird."

"Okay, I'll do that. How's it going, kid? Stayin' busy?"

They chatted about Ash's work, Albert's golf game, and how Lindsey was doing in school before Albert asked the same question he asked every single Sunday.

"So, did you meet anybody yet?" The senior Mr. Riggs wanted his son to find someone and have a good marriage like his own.

"Maybe," was Ash's only reply.

His father's eyes widened and his face lit up. "Really?"

"It's way too soon to tell, but someone has certainly gotten my attention."

"Albert, I could use your help now," Maggie Riggs called from the kitchen.

"Come tell me about this woman while I carve the turkey."

"There's nothing to tell, really. She's not aware that I exist, and I have no idea if she's even available, but she goes to St. Matthews, and I intend to find out."

Ash knew his purpose in going to church was to worship, not to meet a woman, but who ever said you couldn't do both? You never know. That could be God's plan.

Dr. Riggs was suddenly hungry for more than turkey. He had a new appetite. The idea of running into Merry in church was promising, but Sunday was a whole week away, and Ash really hoped he'd run into her again before that. He knew he was being ridiculous—acting like a love-struck school boy, yet he simply couldn't get her out of his mind.

Over dinner, Albert, a doctor himself though he'd retired and sold his private practice a few years earlier, asked Ash how things were going with his favorite patients.

"Most are doing as well as can be expected, some better, but I'm a little concerned about one of my favorite ladies. She's got a birthday coming up—tomorrow, actually—and it's hitting her pretty hard. She's showing signs of major depression."

"How old?"

"Ninety-seven."

"No wonder she's depressed," Lindsey chimed in.

"Careful there, missy," Albert chuckled then added, "I'll be there before you know it. Pass the rolls, please."

"No, you won't, Pap. You're not even close to that," Lindsey said with a mouthful of her grammy's stuffing.

Albert winked at his wife and took a sip of wine before asking Ash, "Do you think your patient needs an antidepressant or is she already on something?"

"No, she hasn't needed one, and I'd rather not go that route if we can avoid it. I got her to go to the dining room for lunch Friday, and that seemed to help." Ash picked up his fork then put it back down. "I think I'll make her birthday something special. I'm sure the rest of the staff and her friends at Vigilant will all be glad to help."

"Great idea, son."

After dinner, the family gathered in the living room to watch one of their favorite holiday movies, *A Christmas Carol*. It was the one with George C. Scott as Scrooge, and they all loved this version, though Lindsey appeared to be watching her phone more than the TV screen.

Ash's mind wandered and his plan to make Miss Tilly feel special on her birthday got legs. They could decorate and surprise her at lunch, and then he got another idea. Maybe after lunch he could take her for a special outing. He'd take her out for coffee at Latte Da.

And you never know who you might run into there.

9 MERRY

"I know not what the future holds,
but I know who holds the future."
                                        —Homer

Monday, December 23

Monday morning, Merry decided to take advantage of the quiet and get most of her work done before Katie and Jimmy got up and broke the silence. She couldn't blame them for sleeping in on the first official day of their school's Christmas holiday. Normally they had to be up, dressed, and fed in time to catch the school bus by 7:15, so she'd let them enjoy the luxury of sleeping late today.

Merry lost track of time, and it was close to one o'clock when the rumbling of her stomach distracted her from the manuscript she was working on. She rubbed her eyes, stretched, and dragged herself to the kitchen for something to eat and another jolt of caffeine.

They can't still be in bed.

They weren't. She found Jimmy devouring the last of the raisin bran at the kitchen table in the nook where they took most of their meals now that Grandma wasn't around, and Katie stood at the counter scooping way too much sugar into a large mug that said "Nacho average teenager." No wonder it was so quiet. The caffeine and fuel hadn't kicked in yet. Merry noticed there was barely enough brew left in the pot for half a cup.

"Now that you've taken to drinking coffee in the morning—or whenever you drag yourself out of bed," she said looking at the clock on the microwave—"you need to learn some coffee etiquette." Merry poured what was left into her mug, dumped the old grounds out, and reached for the last of the French roast. "Never leave the pot so low that there's not enough for the next person... until bedtime, that is."

"Sorry, Mom. Love you." Katie kissed her mother on the cheek and drifted over to the table with coffee in one hand, phone in the other.

"I don't know how you guys drink that stuff." Jimmy shook his head and stuffed another huge spoonful of cereal in his mouth.

"And I don't know how you stuff your face like that, pig boy." Katie dropped the words, and a little slap upside her brother's head before sitting down.

Merry sometimes worried about how much time her daughter spent on her phone, but since she'd discovered that Katie spent more time reading or doing research on it than texting or whatever, her mind was put more at ease.

"All right, you two. Knock it off. Is it safe to leave you guys alone while I run up to Latte Da and get some more coffee?"

She got a "Sure" from Katie and an exaggerated "*Yes*, Mom" from Jimmy, so Merry felt safe leaving, although she knew there was really no need to worry. Her children's squabbles never went beyond verbal arguments and slamming doors. Katie was actually quite protective of her little brother.

"You might try getting dressed before I get back," Merry said, grabbing an apple on her way out the door.

"Okay, and something sweet would sure go great with the coffee... just sayin'."

Katie's sweet tooth would probably bite her in the butt someday, but for now she could get away with it, so Merry would make a quick stop at Emilie's Boulangerie for a few bakery treasures. They were the best in town, and if Merry was going to splurge on calories, it might as well be worth it.

When she got to Latte Da, Bobby asked if she wanted the usual, but she decided to show a little restraint.

"No, I just need beans today. Give me a pound of the French Roast... and a pound of some of the Breakfast Blend too." She would indulge Katie who preferred a milder brew.

She paid for her purchase, turned to leave and, in her hurry, nearly ran into a white-haired lady with a cane in one hand and her purse in the other.

"Oh, I'm so sorry!"

The elderly woman simply smiled at her and then at the tall gentleman at her elbow.

You have got to be kidding.

"Hello, Merry. It's all right. I'm sure she's okay, aren't you, Miss Tilly?"

Miss Tilly nodded and asked, "Do you know this young lady?"

"I've run into her before," Ash said with a wink. "Miss Tilly, this is Merry..." he paused, and Merry finished for him.

"It's Merry Snyder. M-E-R-R-Y." Seeing the elderly woman's quizzical smile, she added, "My parents had prayed for a child for so long, and I was born on Christmas day." *Why am I blathering on?* "My mother says my dad was overjoyed and when he picked me up, she said, 'Merry Christmas, Walt.' That was my father's name. And he said, 'That's what we should name her'." *Stop talking.* "My dad gave me the name Merry and it stuck." *Why can't I shut up?*

"Your name is Merry Christmas?"

"No. I mean my mother drew the line there. She liked the idea for spelling my name m-e-r-r-y, but she added her sister's name, Carol. So I'm Merry Carol. And I'm sorry, I'm rambling—"

"Well, that's a lovely name, dear. My sister's name was Mary Ann." She looked up at Ash. "Did you know that, Dr. Riggs?"

Doctor?

Ash responded softly, but Merry didn't hear what he said, and not knowing what else to add, she stammered about having to get back to her family and hurried out to the car.

It was literally freezing—twenty-six degrees, to be exact—but once in the car, she fanned her burning face and neck. With trembling fingers, she put her key in the ignition and pulled away from the curb without looking back.

She was two blocks from her house when she realized she'd forgotten to stop at Emilie's. "I'm getting more like Mom every day," she said out loud.

Turning right onto Maple Street to head back to the bakery, she couldn't help but wonder if her forgetfulness meant she was heading down the same road as her mother. *Or is it just the Dr. Ash Riggs effect?*

Strange how she'd never laid eyes on this man until four days ago, but now she couldn't seem to get away from him—even if she wanted to.

When she finally got home, the kitchen was empty and the house quiet. The kids obviously hadn't heard her come in, or they would've already been into the box of doughnuts.

After wolfing down one of her own favorites, a chocolate-covered custard-filled delight, Merry meandered into the living room where she found both of her teens busy on their phones. Two sets of earbuds explained why they hadn't come running. Jimmy was sprawled on the sofa, but it was Katie who made Merry catch her breath. There she sat, still in her pajamas, slowly rocking in her grandma's chair. She even had one of her grandma's old shawls wrapped around her.

"I guess nobody wants any of these doughnuts," she said, shaking off her reaction to seeing Katie look so much like her mom.

No response.

Taking a few steps to stand between and in plain view of her kids, Merry held up the box and raised her voice to be heard over whatever YouTube or TikTok nonsense they were listening to.

"Anybody want a doughnut?"

Jimmy was the first one up and in front of her grabbing at the box with Katie right behind him, but they still weren't dressed, and at this rate they'd be in their PJs at the dinner table.

Merry stepped back, holding the box tight to her chest with one hand firmly over the lid.

"What the heck?" Jimmy threw his hand in the air in disgust.

Katie's eyes widened and her eyebrows jumped halfway up her forehead as she stood arms akimbo. "So what's up, Mom? What's the deal?"

"The deal is, the first one dressed gets first pick in the box."

Merry laughed at the immediate disappearing act and was going to take the baked goods back to the kitchen when she noticed her mother's chair still gently rocking with her shawl now tossed aside.

Merry picked it up and held it against her cheek for a few seconds, breathing in the lingering scent of her mother before folding and laying it over the back of the rocker.

10 Ash

Ash knew finding her in a google search was a long shot, and perhaps a bit creepy, but he couldn't help himself. She'd said her last name was Snyder, and there couldn't be that many Snyders with the first name M.E.R.R.Y.

Ash stared at the profile picture of her on Facebook and was relieved to see the image only included her two children. *A son and a daughter.* He was relieved that there wasn't a man in the picture. Of course, that didn't rule out the possibility that there was a man in her life. Her account was private, so he couldn't see any other posts or pictures without sending her a friend request. And that *would* be creepy. *But maybe—*

Dressed and ready for her date with this Elliot kid, Lindsey interrupted his thoughts. "I'm ready."

When he looked up from his tablet, Ash was both pleased and distressed by what he saw. Her perfect, sunny smile more than paid the price for her years in braces, and her blonde bob was like a halo framing his little angel's face. But was she really only seventeen?

Lindsey rarely wore much makeup, but now seeing how her blue eyes drew his attention, he realized she was wearing eyeshadow and liner, and her lips were a shiny pink.

"How do I look?" she asked.

He knew what he should answer despite wanting to tell her she looked too old and too beautiful to be going out with some hormone-filled teenage boy.

"You look great," he managed. "Is that a new top?"

"Yeah. Cool, huh? I got it Saturday when we went to the mall."

"Definitely cool." Ash chuckled. She was wearing jeans and a honey-colored top with a bulky brown sweater that covered her bottom. Ash was pleased with that. "Are those new boots?"

"Sort of. I've had them awhile, but I only wear them for special occasions."

Special occasions... right.

"Well, grab your coat, and I'll drive you."

"I'm good."

"No coat? It's only about thirty degrees out there. You really think you'll be warm enough?"

"Yeah, I'm good." Lindsey hurried out the door with Ash right behind her thinking, *Now it begins.*

***

Ash tried not to resent the time this boy Elliot was stealing from him and reminded himself he and Lindsey would have the whole day to spend together tomorrow. Besides, she'd only be out for a few hours, and he should be used to that. Lindsey often spent time with her best friend, Darcy. He still preferred when the two girls hung out at his place. He'd hear them playing music and singing back in Lindsey's bedroom. His daughter had a great voice and had often sung in musicals at the local children's theater over the years, and she and Darcy harmonized beautifully.

As much as he usually treasured peace and quiet, now the silence seemed to close in on him. Though he'd lived alone all this time—and quite contentedly—he realized what he was feeling was loneliness.

He turned on the TV and searched for a distraction. *The Santa Clause.* That would work. Tim Allen always made him laugh. But Ash found himself struck by the character Laura's resemblance to M.E.R.R.Y. *C'mon man, she doesn't really look like her. They don't even have the same color hair.*

Put them side by side, and there was no contest. "If I could choose, I'd take Merry every time. If only."

Lucky for Ash, when the movie ended, it was time to pick up his daughter. He saw her waiting, and the boy next to her—who he had to admit was a good-looking kid—had his hands in his pockets. They were having an animated conversation which ended with a quick hug when Ash pulled up.

Merry Snyder forgotten, his full attention was on his daughter now. "How was the movie?" he asked when she hopped in the car.

"Huh? Oh, it was pretty good. Hilarious, actually."

"So, you had a good time?"

He could feel his daughter staring at him, and when he ventured a glance her way, he saw the big grin.

"Yes, Pops. I had an excellent time."

Ash knew she was being playful whenever she called him "Pops" instead of Dad, and he couldn't help laughing. Yeah, she was still his little girl.

11 MERRY

*"Christmas is doing a little something extra
for someone." —Charles Schulz*

Even though Katie was the athletic one and excelled in track and field, Jimmy nearly knocked Katie over, managing to win by a nose. Fortunately, he chose the chocolate caramel crunch doughnut, and Katie was all about the maple bacon one.

Her daughter's choice solved Merry's dilemma as she'd been torn between that one and Emilie's latest flavor, the pina colada.

It was obvious by the few minutes of silence in the room that everyone was satisfied with their selection. Jimmy was the first one to finish and was already reaching for a second when Merry caught him by the wrist and gave him the double raised eyebrows.

"Please?"

She couldn't resist Jimmy's big, innocent brown eyes, especially when he batted those long eyelashes any woman would envy. Besides, she could hear her mother's voice saying, *"Oh, let him have another one. He's a growing boy."*

"Go ahead, but just one more."

Jimmy and two of his buddies planned to start a band someday, and Merry could already imagine the girls falling all over her good-looking son.

"Me too?" Katie asked with her mouth full and at least one more bite left in her hand.

Merry nodded. "But you can slow down. They're not going anywhere."

She watched their joyful noshing away and felt her heart swell. She could only imagine how their faces would light up Christmas morning when they got their presents. She couldn't have managed either surprise without Fred's help.

He had finished the work in the basement—and would only accept a fraction of what any other contractor would have charged—and Katie's present was tucked away in the garage next door with Fred's promise to put it in Merry's driveway early Christmas morning.

Both gifts were from Merry and her mom. In her most lucid moments, Virginia Graham had made it clear she wanted to do something special for her grandchildren.

Merry hadn't known the extent of her mother's assets until getting power of attorney. That's when Mom shared her wishes.

"You should hang onto the stocks as long as you can, dear. Jim assures me they're solid, and he'd never lead us astray... never has, never will."

The Grahams had always relied on their accountant, Jim Hathaway, and Jim had guided Mrs. Graham through the labyrinth of paperwork when she was left a widow with a business to sell and little knowledge of their finances.

Because of Merry's father's business and wise investments along with her mother's frugality, Merry was still getting used to the idea that she didn't need to worry about money, and she could give her kids a great Christmas this year and maybe take some of the sting out of seeing the empty place at the table... and the empty rocking chair.

Merry returned to her office and read over the changes she'd made to the latest manuscript earlier in the day. Satisfied with the result, she opened her email and sent it on its way to her publisher, then grabbed her notebook to see if there was anything else she had to do before putting work aside until Thursday. She was determined not to look at, or even think about work on Christmas Eve or Christmas Day. She might not be able to make this Christmas a great one, but she remained resolute that she would not spoil it for her children.

Seeing nothing more that couldn't wait, Merry sank back into her chair, and looked at the next blank lined page in her tablet, then began to write.

Dr. Ash Riggs. Merry Riggs. Dr. & Mrs. Riggs

Wow, I'm losing it. What am I, a fifteen-year-old? Stop it!

"Hey Mom, what's for dinner?" Jimmy leaned in, hands on either side of the doorway. "Can we get Chinese?"

"Sure. I guess." Merry had planned to make spaghetti but now realized she hadn't gotten the ground beef out of the freezer for the sauce. "It's a little early though. You can't be hungry for dinner already."

"I can, but nah, just thinking ahead." Merry heard him call to his sister, "She said okay, but you have to ask her if you can go pick it up yourself."

Merry couldn't hear Katie's response, but she wasn't surprised that her seventeen-year-old wanted to run for their dinner. *I may never see her once she has her own car.*

Maybe this Christmas would be okay, but without Grandma...

Merry closed her notebook and put it in the center desk drawer, then meandered out to the family room where her kids sat on either end of the sofa, eyes glued to their phones. She stared at her mother's rocking chair, ran her hand lovingly across the top, then eased herself into it and rocked, staring at the fireplace. Tomorrow she would have Jimmy lay a fire for Christmas Eve, but now it sat looking empty and cold, much like she felt.

Then she had an idea. "Hey Jimmy, come give me a hand with this chair."

"What d'ya mean?"

"Help me carry it out to the car."

"Where are you going with Grandma's chair?" Katie's eyes went wide with the question.

"Nowhere today, but tomorrow it's going to go to someone who will really appreciate it." *This is the perfect gift.*

12 Ash

*"It is Christmas in the heart
that puts Christmas in the air."
—William Thomas Ellis*

Tuesday, December 24

Ash was perusing the never-ending list of emails—delete, move to folder, flag—when he was interrupted by his daughter's excited shout coming down the hall.

"Look, Dad. It's snowing!" She dashed to the window.

He looked at the time and chuckled. "And you're awake to see it at nine o'clock in the morning. Remarkable."

He looked at his seventeen-year-old daughter and saw the same dimpled little girl grin he'd fallen in love with when she was a toddler. The dimple was the only feature she'd gotten from him. It was as though God had taken that exact defect from Ash's face and placed in a miniature of her mother's blue-eyed, heart-shaped face and found perfection. Ash even loved the pink highlights his daughter had added to her silky blonde locks.

"Hey, it's Christmas Eve, which is our Christmas. No time to waste."

Now Lindsey was laughing. "How soon do you want to leave?"

"How soon can you be ready?"

Lindsey vanished down the hall and Ash wondered when he'd last seen her move so fast. "Better dress warm, Linds!" he called.

Lindsey reappeared wearing what her father was sure couldn't possibly be warm enough, but she was seventeen.

"I'm ready. C'mon Dad, don't drag your feet."

The flurries they'd watched falling moments earlier turned into big fluffy flakes that melted on streets and sidewalks but began to gently coat all that was green.

Ash drove to their first traditional stop—the IHOP across town—and ordered their Christmas morning breakfast. He splurged with the eggs benedict, and shook his head watching plates filled with a combo of sausage, eggs, hashbrowns, and a Cinn-A-Stack for Lindsey's endless appetite. Sipping another coffee, he watched as she ate with abandon and was tickled by the whipped topping on her hot chocolate.

They chatted easily as they talked about their plans for the rest of the day. Ash was looking forward to their visit to Vigilant later. This would be the third year Lindsey would come with him to see all the residents and give out the gifts he'd gotten. The BMW was already loaded with several boxes, cards, and special treats depending on each patient's dietary needs.

But first they would share their personal Christmas for two. Ash knew it was nothing like Christmas at her mother's where every inch of space would be decorated with elegant greenery, wreaths, garlands, and silver and gold ornaments. Fran and Rodney's house could be featured in *Better Homes and Gardens*.

With simpler taste, and much less time for decorating, his own home—the one where he and Fran had raised their daughter—was much more to Ash's liking. He didn't need all the expensive décor. Between the few special ornaments Fran hadn't confiscated in the divorce and the fun ones he and Lindsey had added over the last few years, the little tree in the corner of their family room looked perfect to him.

What completed it was when they got back home and, like every year, Lindsey sat cross-legged on the floor beside it ripping open her presents. Fran had emailed him a wish list for their daughter so he had all the right sizes of jeans, shirts, long skirts, sneakers, and accessories. Then there were little boxes with earrings and such.

Each gift brought exclamations of, "Thank you!" "Oh, I love it!" and "Thanks, Dad!" But her biggest surprise would come later.

When she'd opened the final gift under the tree and with no signs of exhaustion—though Ash was tired just watching and gathering up the wrapping paper she tossed aside—Lindsey bolted from the room and reappeared holding several boxes in her arms.

"Merry Christmas!" she said, plonking them on his lap.

Ash took his time opening the gifts from his daughter, enjoying the joy on Lindsey's face even more than the gifts and her thoughtfulness in getting them.

There was a box of personalized golf balls, a butter-yellow golf shirt, and a golf game they could play together on the Xbox he'd gotten them last Christmas. But the gift he loved most was the last one he opened, a framed portrait of his beautiful daughter.

"Could you get me a cup of coffee?" Ash asked, and as soon as Lindsey disappeared into the kitchen, he bolted back to his bedroom closet and pulled out one more gift that had been too much of a challenge to wrap.

He raced back to the family room and was sitting on the sofa next to a Yamaha FG800 with a big red bow around its neck when Lindsey returned with two large mugs in her hands. He had searched for just the right guitar for his petite daughter's small hands and been assured this would be the perfect fit.

Lindsey managed to set the mugs down without spilling a drop before falling onto the couch and caressing the guitar, then throwing her arms around her dad with boundless gratitude. Soon she was strumming and singing, filling the room with music.

Ash wasn't sure he'd be able to tear his daughter away from her new guitar, and he was enjoying the laid-back time as much as she was, but if he wanted to finish his gift-giving at Vigilant Care before the residents began their early dinner, he knew it was time to go.

Surprisingly, Lindsey relinquished the instrument and agreed enthusiastically.

"I can play some more when we get back."

"Be careful," Ash said as his daughter raced to the car. "It's starting to get a little slick." There was no wind, but Ash hurried to get out of the cold, frosty air, and he wondered if the weatherman's prediction of no significant accumulation would be accurate. Lindsey on the other hand seemed immune to the cold as she strolled the final few yards to the BMW.

The roads to the retirement home were wet, not icy, so they arrived in twenty minutes, and Ash pulled into his reserved parking space, hopped out, and went to grab one of the boxes he'd filled with gifts earlier in the day.

He was about to call to his daughter to come grab the other box when, out of the corner of his eye, he saw her rushing past him.

"That lady fell!" she called over her shoulder.

Ash whipped around, fearing the worst. Did one of his patients venture out and fall on the ice? He could envision a broken hip or worse.

Reaching for his phone to possibly call 911 while hastening behind his daughter, Ash was relieved to see Lindsey and several other young people trying to help a woman up. His anxiety eased when he saw brown rather than gray or white hair, and his jaw dropped when he finally saw the woman's face. *Merry!*

He saw her sitting on the slippery wet ground between two cars and the anxiety rushed back. "Are you all right? Maybe you shouldn't move."

When she looked up his heart quickened.

Merry snickered. "You again? I'm okay." She struggled, trying to find a way to get herself up. "Only thing hurt is my pride."

She managed to get one knee under her and searched for something to grab hold of. She found a surprisingly warm man's hand.

"You sure you're not hurt, Mom?" one of the two teens asked.

Ash recognized the girl but hadn't seen this boy at church with Merry, and he couldn't help wondering if there was an older version of the kid waiting at home.

With her son on one side and Ash on the other, they helped Merry to her feet.

"I told you I could get it myself," the boy insisted.

"Do you need help with something?" Ash watched as the kid started dragging a rocking chair out of the back of their vehicle.

"No, I've got it, thanks."

Ash noticed Merry rubbing her hip, and she was obviously having trouble putting weight on her right leg.

"Are you certain you're not hurt, Merry? Is it your ankle?" *After all*, he thought, *you don't have to be elderly to get hurt.*

"Yes, I'm sure." Merry leaned against the car. "Probably just gonna be a little black and blue tomorrow. What are you doing here anyway?"

"Oh, I work here. My daughter and I came to hand out gifts to the residents."

Introductions were made all around before Ash suggested they get out of the weather. He helped Jimmy carry the old rocking chair inside, and watched Merry hanging onto her daughter and limping along in front of them.

Once inside, he insisted Merry sit down in one of the easy chairs near the entrance while he examined her ankle.

"I don't think it's sprained, but you should probably put some ice on it."

"Thanks. I'll be fine."

Merry's daughter helped her up, and Ash watched as the woman he couldn't stop thinking about hobbled across the lobby. He quickly looked away when he saw her glance back in his direction.

"Dad?"

"Yeah, Linds," he said before hurrying back to his vehicle for the nearly forgotten boxes. Meanwhile, his mind was spinning. Ash wasn't one to believe in fate, but could this really be a coincidence?

He didn't think so.

13 ᴹᴇʀʀʏ

"It's Christmas Eve. It's the one night of the year when we all act a little nicer, we smile a little easier, we cheer a little more. For a couple of hours out of the whole year we are the people that we always hoped we would be."

—Scrooged

"This can't be a coincidence," Merry said to herself.

"What'd you say, Mom?" Jimmy had come up behind her.

"Oh, nothing. I was talking to myself. I guess that's what one does after making a fool out of oneself."

Jimmy laughed but then asked if she was sure she was okay. He and Katie both still looked concerned. Once she had reassured them, they went back to the task at hand, and she looked back out at the parking area.

Merry watched Ash and his daughter hurrying back to his car and absently rubbed her bottom before turning to follow Jimmy and Katie who were lugging the rocking chair down the hall in front of her. She knew that spot in the family room would look empty without it, but it would serve a greater purpose here.

All thoughts of the doctor's maple syrup eyes were pushed aside as they went through the door into room #104. A white-haired woman, impeccably groomed, sat by the window with a Bible in her lap and stared blankly at the intruders, no recognition in her eyes.

"Hi Mom," Merry said. "Merry Christmas. We brought you a present." Virginia Graham looked like the same woman she'd always been, except for her eyes. The sharp blue had grown dull. Merry bent down, cupped her mother's chin, and kissed her on the forehead, praying for some kind of recognition, especially today. Especially on Christmas Eve.

"Katie and Jimmy are here, Mom," she said, searching the older woman's eyes.

"Hi, Grandma," came in unison as each of the teens hugged her in turn, but Virginia searched each face looking perplexed.

Her gaze landed on her beloved rocking chair, and for a moment, Merry thought she saw a glimmer of recognition. Getting to her feet easily—other than a little arthritis she was physically in good shape—she approached the chair, slid her hand across the back and down the side, then lowered herself into it and began to rock.

"This is lovely," she said. "Thank you, Miss?"

The question in her voice and her eyes crushed Merry. *She doesn't know us.*

"It's me, Mom... Merry."

Her mother looked bewildered and began to ring her hands.

It's all right, Mom. Merry changed the subject to ease her mother's anxiety. "It's Christmas Eve and the kids and I thought you might like some Christmas music." She nodded to Katie who pulled out her phone and cued up the music.

As the song began, Virginia closed her eyes and her lips curved into a slow smile. Merry and Katie began singing along. Jimmy had warned earlier that he couldn't do it. Maybe he'd just hum along or something, but it was Grandma who began humming softly as Merry and Katie sang along with Josh Groban.

> O Holy Night! The stars are brightly shining
> It is the night of our dear Savior's birth
> Long lay the world in sin and error pining
> 'Til He appears and the soul felt its worth

Softly at first, but stronger with every note, Mrs. Graham joined in. Merry gasped and her throat tightened, but she managed to sing on.

> A thrill of hope the weary world rejoices

And Merry's heart soared. She saw tears sliding down Katie's cheeks, and Jimmy had turned discreetly away.

When they got to the last line of the first verse, Merry, who couldn't reach the high notes, lip-synced, but her mother's voice grew stronger.

After the final note, Virginia patted her daughter's hand. "You never could reach those high notes."

Merry's head snapped up. "Mom?"

Her mother looked back at her, full recognition in her eyes.

"Merry Christmas," she said. "It's so wonderful to see you." Rising from her rocking chair, she embraced first her daughter, then her grandchildren. "You brought my favorite chair. Oh, I've missed this rocker, but won't you miss it now?"

Not as much as we miss you. "It's your chair, Mom. It belongs with you. We want you to enjoy it."

"Did I hear a chorus of angels in here?" Dr. Ashley Riggs stood in the doorway with a beautifully wrapped gift in his hands. "Oh, it's you," he said to Merry, looking incredulous. "Do you know this lovely lady?" he asked.

"She's my mom." Merry's heart started pounding like it wanted to pop out of her chest. She put her arm around her mother and pulled her close.

"Wow, small world. She's one of my favorite patients, right Miss Ginny?"

"Oh now, didn't you tell me I was your girlfriend this morning?"

It had actually been days earlier, but her memory signaled her return to the present, at least for now.

"Our little Christmas miracle," Merry murmured softly.

"I can't think of a better gift," the doctor said. "Looks like you were just the medicine my patient needed."

"Now what are you two whispering about?"

"We were just saying how wonderful it is to be with your family at Christmas, Mom."

Ash offered the gift he'd been holding. "Well, I don't want to interrupt your family visit. I just wanted to wish you a Merry Christmas."

Virginia took the present he offered, carefully removed the bow which she placed on top of her head with a mischievous grin, and peeled open the gift wrap. When she opened the box and turned back the tissue paper, she lifted the white pashmina to her cheek. "It's so soft." She gently unfolded it, and with her granddaughter's help, put it around her shoulders. "This is so thoughtful, doctor. Thank you!"

Merry laid a hand over her heart and smiled at Ash, hoping he could see how much she appreciated his kindness.

"Well, I'd best go rescue my daughter from Happy Jack's antics. We need to be on our way to our next stop. I'll see you Friday, Miss Ginny." He looked from his patient to her daughter. "Merry Christmas!"

Virginia laughed. "Tell Jack I said Merry Christmas."

After her doctor left, Merry's mother became quiet, and with a smile on her face, closed her eyes and rocked. Merry watched her for several minutes before she nervously whispered, "Mom?"

"Yes, I'm still here, dear."

A sigh of relief escaped Merry's lips, and she saw her mother open one eye to sneak a look at her.

"How are you doing, Merry?" her mother asked, now leaning forward in her chair with both eyes opened. "Is everything okay at the house? Are Fred and Judy looking out for you?"

"I'm fine, Mom, and yes, they've been wonderful. Fred's finished Jimmy's Christmas present," she added, whispering behind her hand. Noticing her mother's blank expression, Merry decided to let that topic go. "Besides I've got these two monkeys. We're all fine, but... we miss you. I... I wish..."

"Now, now dear. I'm right here. I understand it's hard, but we talked about this." Virginia paused, nodding her head and folding her hands. "We knew it would be difficult, and I'm sorry to put you through all this. I—"

"No! Mom, don't worry about us. We're good. Right, kids?"

Jimmy and Katie quickly agreed, and launched into tales of things they've been up to. Katie excitedly told her about how well she could drive now, and Jimmy talked about his music.

Merry watched in amazement, hardly believing how with-it Virginia Graham was in this moment. She knew it probably wouldn't last too long, but she'd take it. It was the best Christmas gift she could have hoped for.

"Are you and your family coming down to dinner, Miss Ginny?" a volunteer asked from the doorway.

"Can you stay, dear?" Virginia asked.

"Of course, Mom. We'll stay as long as you want."

With a cane in her right hand, Virginia took her daughter's arm with her left. "Why so glum, Merry?"

"No, no, I'm fine."

"Merry?"

"Okay," she said watching Katie and Jimmy walk ahead of them looking nearly grown. "Yeah, I do miss you... a lot. It's hard to get used to you not being there with us. Sometimes the old house just feels kind of empty. Like tomorrow... Christmas. It won't be quite the same without you there, you know? I want it to be perfect, but—"

"Of course you do. But Merry, it will be perfect." Virginia stopped walking and turned to her daughter. She hooked the cane over the arm she had resting on Merry's, and put her palm on her daughter's chest. "It's what's in your heart that makes it perfect." She raised her hand to her daughter's cheek then stroked her hair.

All the times her mother had been there with love and support came rushing back to Merry. When she was ten years old and fell off her bike and broke her arm, when she was a teenager whose first love had broken her heart, when she was a young mother left alone to raise two little children. Her mother had always been there for her and always knew exactly what to say and do.

If only I could be more like her.

"But I could never pull off the flawless perfection you did, Mom. You've always made Christmas Day magical."

Virginia chuckled. "Is that how you remember it? How nice," she said placing the tip of her cane on the floor ahead of her. "And that's how Katie and Jimmy will remember what you do, Merry. They won't recall, or even notice, the little things you might miss or forget. They'll remember how special you made the day. They'll remember the love you put into it, nothing else."

"You always know how to make me feel better, Mom. I still wish you could be there with us."

"I will be... always." She grabbed the cane again and moved forward. "Every time you sing 'O Holy Night,' I want you to hear me singing with you. I'll get the high notes." She winked.

Merry felt the knot in her throat grow and could only respond by squeezing her mother's hand.

The four of them sat at a large table with several patients Virginia seemed to know (at least for now), and they all listened to Jimmy and Katie's animated chatter.

It wasn't until right before dessert that Merry thought she noticed a slight change. Her mother was talking to a lady she called Patsy who obviously struggled with memory.

"And who did you say these people are?" she asked.

Virginia gave her daughter a quizzical look. "What's your name again, dear?"

"Merry. It's Merry, Mom." She watched as her mother began wringing her hands and saw how her gaze bounced from place to place.

"I'm tired. Could you walk me back to my room please, nurse?"

"Of course, Miss Ginny."

***

The drive home was quiet with a mix of joy and melancholy leaving the three Snyders with little to say. Even though they'd had an early dinner with Grandma, the December sun was setting. It's reflection on the fresh snow was magical.

It's Christmas Eve. The holiest night of the year.

"Hey, Mom." Katie was watching her from the passenger seat.

"Hmm?"

"So that doctor guy? Wasn't he like the same guy you saw at church?"

At the store, buying my coffee, in church, and now here... Mom's doctor.

"Yep, same guy." Merry wondered why her heart quickened at the mention of him, and her mind juggled the ideas of luck, chance, happenstance... or could it be fate? *Why does God keep crossing our paths?*

14 Ash

"Okay Linds, are you ready to go see Grammy and Pap?" Ash had given out the last of his Christmas presents and his heart was full—full of the kind of love you only get by giving.

"What?" Lindsey gave her father a quizzical look.

"What do you mean 'what'?"

"I mean, what are you grinning about?"

"Oh, I was just thinking about Happy Jack's reaction when he opened his gift."

They both chuckled at the memory.

"Yeah, I can't believe anyone can get that excited about socks."

"That's because you've never experienced the misery of living with cold feet."

"So tell me this, Dad. Why is he always so happy?"

"I asked him about that once, and you know what he said?"

"What?"

"He said he chooses it each morning." Ash shook his head and smiled. "Yeah, he told me he figured out a long time ago that life was a lot better that way than being miserable focusing on what ails ya." Ash had been guiding his daughter toward the door, but when he pulled it open and stepped to the side for Lindsey to pass, something caught his eye.

There was possibly the most beautiful woman he'd ever seen limping down the hall with the lovely Miss Ginny. Ash watched in wonder until Merry disappeared into her mother's room.

"Dad?"

"Yes, I'm coming." He hurried out to the car with his daughter and with the memory of Merry.

***

Ash and Lindsey had filled their plates at his parents' buffet and were eating cookies and watching *The Santa Clause*, but Ash's mind kept wandering back to Vigilant and Merry. So, she was Miss Ginny's daughter. Happy coincidence, or answered prayers?

Whatever it was, he was ready to accept it. He wouldn't turn his back on this chance for the kind of happiness he hadn't even known he longed for.

15 MERRY

> *"One of the most glorious messes in the world is the mess created in the living room on Christmas Day. Don't clean it up too quickly."*
>
> —Andy Rooney

Wednesday, December 25

Katie and Jimmy collected all the shredded wrapping paper and stuffed it into the large trash bag.

"Katie, would you take that out to the garage and get it out of the way, please?"

"Me?"

"Yes, please." Merry understood the quizzical look on her daughter's face. Jimmy was the one who always took the trash out to the cans in the garage. "I have something else I need Jimmy to help me with."

Katie gathered up the bag and headed through the kitchen toward the door to the garage.

"What do you need me to do, Mom?" Jimmy asked.

"Shh, follow me," Merry whispered.

Katie had tossed the big bag into the large trash can when her mother hit the button to open the garage. Katie spun around at the sound and her eyes seemed to double in size.

Her head whipped around and her jaw dropped. "No way!" She ran to the driver's side door of the arctic blue Volkswagen parked in the driveway. "Seriously, I mean for real? You got me a punch buggy? It's mine?"

"That big red bow on the front sure looks like a Christmas present to me." Merry dangled the keys in front of her and laughed when they were snatched from her hand.

Katie dashed to the car then flew back and threw her arms around her mother's neck. "Thank you, thank you, thank you!"

"It's from Grandma too," Merry said, but Katie was already hopping into the driver's seat with Jimmy running to the passenger side. He seemed to be almost as excited as his sister. She would explain it all to them later.

"Jerkface!" she heard Katie call her brother when he hit her arm calling "punch buggy," but then she laughed. "You better be careful if you want me to drive you to school."

Katie was obviously disappointed when Merry asked her to wait awhile before taking it out for a ride, but Santa wasn't quite finished yet.

Back inside, she could see Jimmy was doing his best not to show his envy, but Merry knew her son had to be feeling like he got the short end of the stick. She hadn't thought of any clever way to get him downstairs, and she didn't want to miss the look on his face when he saw what Fred had created for him, so she decided to make it simple.

"Come on downstairs with me, kids. There's something I want to show you."

At the bottom of the stairs, Merry glanced over her shoulder and saw the surprise and curiosity on her children's faces when they came face to face with a wall that hadn't been there the last time they'd ventured down to the basement.

"What the heck?" Jimmy said.

"C'mon," she said reaching for the door. Jimmy was right behind her, and she guessed he suspected something now. "Merry Christmas, Jimmy."

Merry stepped aside to watch her son's face. His gaze went around the room and back to his mother, and a slow grin seemed to take over his entire face.

"What?" He laughed, frozen in place. "Holy shi... I mean holy cow! How? I mean..." Jimmy's voice drifted off as he moved around the new soundproof room, touching the walls, examining the sound system.

"Your grandma and I have been wanting to do this for you, and thanks to Mr. Fred's help, maybe you won't be driving us out of the house when you guys practice."

In a flash, Jimmy was plugged in and hitting his favorite chords.

"Katie," Merry covered her ears and called. "Let's see how this soundproofing works."

Reaching the top of the stairs, Katie, who was still clutching the keys to her new car, begged, "Now, Mom?"

"Go ahead."

Merry watched her daughter back her blue bug out of the garage and caught herself humming, "We wish you a Merry Christmas." She had done it. She had made this a special Christmas for her kids even though Grandma wasn't there. And they had made it special for her.

It wasn't so much by how her children had saved their money and gone together to buy her a beautiful pair of turquoise earrings for her birthday, or the necklace they said was for Christmas, and not even the beautiful birthday cake they'd gotten from Emilie's—though all of those things meant the world to her and made her feel so loved—but it was the looks on their faces—the joy they expressed—that seemed to say, "Yeah, Mom, you did okay."

It was strange standing alone in Virginia's kitchen, a kitchen that had barely changed since Jimmy and Katie had chased each other from the entry into the living room, through the dining room, into the kitchen and through the nook back to the entry. Round and round and round they'd go giggling all the way until Merry or Virginia would catch them up.

Staring out over the terrace and the last traces of yesterday's snowfall, Merry felt suddenly alone. That feeling of something missing... her thoughts were interrupted by the sound of the doorbell.

"Who in the world?"

Deciding it could only be Fred and Judy stopping in with Christmas greetings, she hurried to let them in. But she did not see the familiar friendly faces of her next-door neighbors.

There in her doorway stood the gorgeous hunk of a man she'd once thought of only as Jerkface, and leaning on his arm was the most beautiful sight she could have seen.

"Mom!"

Hugs and tears were followed by questions. Especially how?

Dr. Riggs explained he was alone since his daughter was spending Christmas Day with her mother, so before going to spend some time with his own mother and father, he decided to stop in and see some of his favorite patients.

"I found Miss Ginny here up, dressed, and a bit restless. It seems she was missing you and the kids... so we decided to take a little field trip."

"Mom, I love it!"

"Grandma!" Back from driving her new wheels, Katie ran to give her grandmother a hug. "Why didn't you tell us Grandma was coming?"

"I didn't know." Merry was still in shock herself.

Katie helped her grandmother to a seat and babbled on about how much she loved her new car and Jimmy absolutely loved his room downstairs while Virginia smiled and nodded and looked happier and more alive than Merry had seen her in a long time.

"We can't stay long, Merry, and I hope you don't mind that I brought her without calling you first." Ash's gaze went back and forth between mother and daughter. "She wanted to surprise you."

"Mind? Are you kidding? I can't thank you enough." Merry saw his shoulders relax with relief. Even his face softened with a more relaxed smile.

"Splendid," he said. "I was surprised to find her completely lucid again this morning and thought you should have this time together."

"I appreciate it, I really do, but I'm sure this isn't how you expected to spend your Christmas."

"I can't think of anyplace I'd rather be right now." Ash draped his arm over her shoulders. "Besides, I'm beginning to think fate has plans for us."

Merry smiled and looked up into his eyes. "I kind of feel like I'm in one of those hokey Hallmark Christmas movies."

Ash chuckled and gave her shoulder a gentle squeeze. "And we know how they always end."

Merry looked from Ash to the scene in the living room where her mother was sandwiched between her grandchildren. Jimmy had torn himself away from his music and was thanking his grandmother for the wonderful gift. She wondered if perhaps what Ash suggested could really be happening. For now, she just wanted to drink in this moment and remember this feeling forever.

Though she might not know the future, there was one thing she knew for sure. Her mother was right... It didn't matter about the cookies or decorations or anything but this. Family. The people you love... and those you are going to love.

THE END

Acknowledgments

Many thanks to my husband for all his encouragement and support, to Kathleen Shoop for teaching a wonderful class that has helped me continue to hone my craft, and as always, to my dear friend, editor, and publisher, Demi Stevens, who always gets me to the finish line.

About the Author

Gloria Bostic is a retired special education teacher from York, Pennsylvania. As a Masters level clinical psychologist, she also worked with women and children to help them overcome abuse. She lives in Dover, PA, with her husband, Lee, and enjoys spending time with her three sons and all her grandchildren.

ALSO BY GLORIA BOSTIC...

Deception Bridge (Book 1)

Valerie Reed is plagued by migraines, insomnia, and a growing anxiety that her happily-ever-after is about to come crumbling down. Tormented by the fear of losing her husband of nearly thirty years, she hangs onto the one thing she knows she can count on – her friendship with the women in her bridge group. They provide a safe-haven with warmth, laughter, and trust... until that trust is broken.

As Val searches for a way to save her marriage and learn to trust again, her life and her bridge group go through unanticipated transformations. Their lives will never be the same, and Val wonders if the power of prayer will be enough to save them all.

Broken Contracts (Book 2)

Through faith and forgiveness Valerie and Andy Reed's marriage has survived and grown stronger in spite of Andy's brief affair five years ago. However, the consequences of his tryst with Susan Walters, a former member of Val's bridge group, may now turn their world upside-down once again.

As Susan's marriage falls apart, all she wants is to be a good mother to the child she had always longed for... yet her life is becoming unmanageable as she continually succumbs to the need for her next drink.

When Valerie, Bonnie, Sarah, and Kathy gather around the bridge table, they share more than the game. Only time will tell what's in the cards.

Premonition Bridge (Book 3)

A threat... A former client warns that her husband is wildly angry that she left him and blames her therapist, Sarah Reed, for ruining his life. He vows to get even.

A disappearance... A member of the Reed family mysteriously disappears without a trace. The only clues to the victim's whereabouts may come from mystifying messages in drawings and dreams.

A reuniting... Family members separated, relationships lost, friendships dissolved... Will prayer and forgiveness be enough for the bridge club ladies to find resolution from the chaos that has invaded their lives?

Out of the Storm

Greta Friedman travels from victim to victory in this story of a young woman's search for the life she's been denied. A childhood filled with loss and abuse leaves her desperate to find love and normalcy, but as a young adult Greta is frustrated by unanswered prayers and a pattern of relationships that end badly... until she meets someone special. When Gabe Engel mysteriously comes into her life, Greta begins the journey that will give her the strength to escape impending danger and finally make her dreams a reality.

Watercolor Whispers (Book 1)

Art therapist Mia Reed has a calling to help her patients as well as a special gift... paintings that unlock mysteries and help solve crimes. However, Freddie Alessi—an assault victim whose wife has gone missing—leaves every session more disturbed than when he arrived... almost as disturbed as Mia feels about his charming and attractive older brother Anthony. Her brain says run, but his fervent kisses keep drawing her back.

Detective Ron Bishop is intrigued by Mia's gift as he struggles to solve missing persons and murder cases. But when Mia's hand is guided by an outside force, can the clues in her drawings lead to the killer and answer the questions in time?

Whispered Warnings (Book 2)

Mia Reed's artwork is a gift from a higher power and holds clues that help solve mysteries. Detective Ronald Bishop, the man she loves, is desperate to find his twin sister who disappeared fifteen years ago. But in the meantime he's lured to follow Mia to her hometown, where a clinical psychologist has jumped to her death. Or did she? When two more single women suffer the same fate, everyone realizes these are not suicides. A serial killer has invaded their peaceful small town! Will Mia's gift help them catch a murderer before he strikes too close to home?

Waiting for the Whisper (Book 3)

Mia's faith is shaken when she discovers a long-held family secret about her family's rock—her beloved grandfather. When she longs to lean on her fiancé, Detective Ron Bishop, for support, his attention is more focused on collecting evidence to prove her client's guilt. Meanwhile he's also hunting down the men who murdered his parents and held his sister Robin captive for years.

Mia understands that putting the kidnappers away is the only thing that will end Robin's nightmare of fear, but she wonders if Ron will ever be there for her again as the clock ticks down to their wedding day. Will Ron's sudden concern for his twin stand in the way of their "happily-ever-after?"

Christmas Melody (novella)

When Ken Patterson dies unexpectedly, his wife and children struggle to get through the holidays. Teenaged Melody can no longer sing in the choir with the joy of the Hallelujah. The only song in her heart is filled with melancholy. Will joy ever return to Melody's song?

The Greatest Aunt

It's a scary time for Flora when she learns her parents must go away. She will have to go live with her great-aunt, but can't understand why they call her great. Flora happily discovers why and agrees!

www.ingramcontent.com/pod-product-compliance
Lightning Source LLC
Chambersburg PA
CBHW030438120726
47903CB00003B/1015